Table of Contents

Once Upon a Princess

Once upon a time, in the kingdom of Enchancia, there lived a little girl named Sofia. She and her mother, Miranda, didn't have much but their cobbler shop, but they were happy.

One morning, Sofia and her mother went to the castle to bring King Roland a new pair of shoes. He and Miranda took one look at each other, and it was love at first sight.

The couple married, and soon Sofia and her mom were off to the castle for a life they never could have imagined.

Miranda lovingly greeted the king's children, Princess Amber and Prince James. King Roland placed a tiara on Sofia's head. "Welcome to the family!" he said warmly.

At dinner that evening, Sofia counted six different forks by her plate! Silverware clattered to the floor as she picked up one fork, then another.

King Roland could see it was going to take a while for Sofia to get used to her new royal life. He had a surprise to help her feel welcome. "We will be throwing a royal ball in your honor at week's end," he said. "And you and I shall dance the first waltz."

Later in Sofia's mom's room, Sofia said, "I don't know how
to be a princess. And I don't know how to dance."

Miranda smiled down at Sofia and assured her daughter
she'd be fine if she just tried her best.

Just then, they heard a knock at the door.

It was King Roland—with a beautiful gift for Sofia!

"It's a very special amulet," he told her. "So you must promise to never take it off. Now you best run off to bed. You have princess school in the morning."

Princess school! Sofia liked the sound of that.

As Sofia skipped back to her room, she bumped into Cedric. The royal sorcerer's beady eyes spotted the amulet. It was the Amulet of Avalor—the powerful charm Cedric had been trying to get for years! With its magic, he could rule Enchancia. Cedric began to scheme how he'd trick Sofia into giving it to him.

The next morning, the headmistresses of Royal Prep Academy—Flora, Fauna, and Merryweather—greeted Sofia at the Academy gates.

Sofia's classmates liked her a lot—which made Amber jealous. She was used to being the popular one!

Amber turned to James. "I think it's time Sofia took a ride on the magic swing."

So James led Sofia to the swing. "Try it! It swings itself."
Sofia climbed onto the swing. The swing suddenly sped up
and sent her flying into the fountain! Sofia put on a brave
smile while the other kids laughed, but James could tell she
was upset. He felt terrible about tricking his new sister.

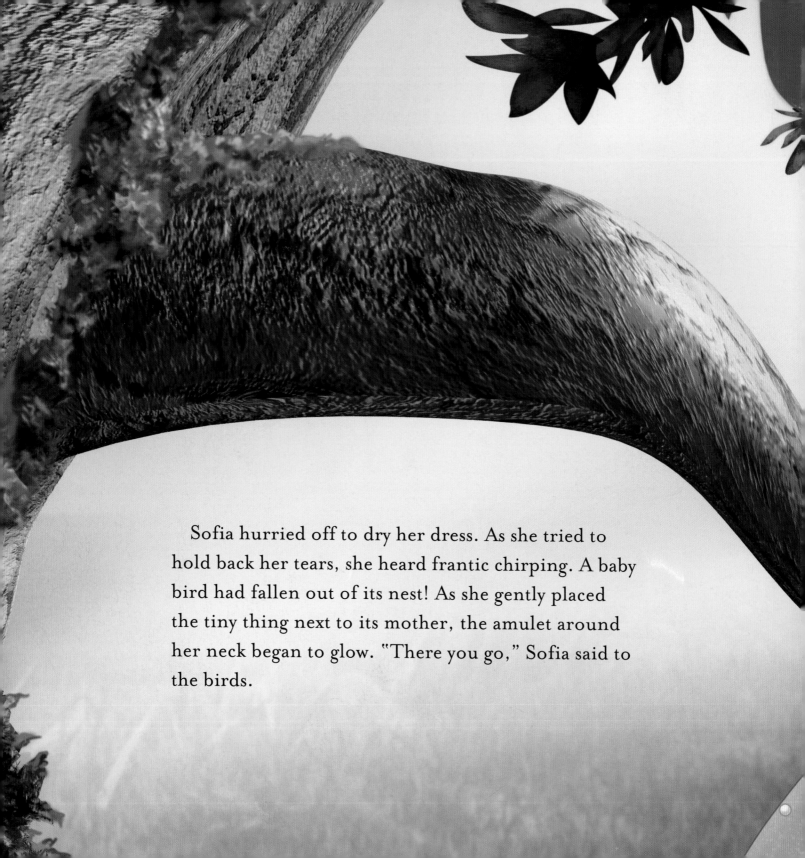

Sofia hurried off to dry her dress. As she tried to hold back her tears, she heard frantic chirping. A baby bird had fallen out of its nest! As she gently placed the tiny thing next to its mother, the amulet around her neck began to glow. "There you go," Sofia said to the birds.

When Sofia turned to leave, she thought she heard a tiny, squeaky voice say "Thank you." But she must have been hearing things. Birds didn't talk!

When Sofia arrived home, Cedric was waiting. "How would you like a private tour of my lair—I mean, workshop?" he asked Sofia.

In Cedric's workshop, Sofia saw a picture of the Amulet of Avalor. "That looks just like my amulet!" she said.

"The Amulet of Avalor contains powerful magic. I can take a quick look at your amulet," Cedric said slyly.

Sofia shook her head. "I promised never to take it off."

As soon as Cedric saw his plan wasn't working, he rushed her out the door. This was going to be tougher than he thought.

The next morning, Sofia awoke to find Clover, a rabbit, and his bird friends Robin and Mia on her bed. Sofia could understand every word they were saying! The amulet gave Sofia the power to talk to animals!

After breakfast with her new friends, Sofia left for Royal Prep. She hoped her second day would be better!

Sofia tried hard in all her classes, but she went home feeling discouraged again. "I thought being a princess would be easy," she sighed to her mother. "But it's really hard."

Miranda had a surprise. Sofia's two best friends, Jade and Ruby, were waiting at a fancy table set for tea!

James joined the party, too. He still felt bad about tricking Sofia and wanted to make it up to her.

Soon Sofia was curtsying and pouring tea like a proper
princess, but she told James she still didn't know how to dance.

"No problem," he assured her. "We have dance class with
Professor Popov tomorrow."

Amber had been watching everyone have fun without her.
Now she was even more jealous of her stepsister. She had to
make sure Sofia didn't dance better than she did!

The next day, before dance class, Amber gave Sofia a
sparkling pair of dance slippers to wear.

Sofia put on the slippers, which immediately took control
of her feet. She spun helplessly across the floor, and collapsed
into a pile of pillows.

"Oh, Sofia! I must have grabbed a pair of Cedric's trick
shoes by mistake. Sorry about that," Amber said with a smile.

Sofia decided she couldn't chance another disaster at the ball. When she got home, she went straight to Cedric for help. He gave Sofia a magic spell to say when the waltz began. Little did she know that the spell would put everyone to sleep and then Cedric could steal the amulet!

Soon it was time for the ball. James came into Amber's room.

"You gave Sofia the trick shoes on purpose," he said angrily. "You're trying to ruin her ball because everyone likes her more than you. And after what you did today, so do I!"

"James! Come back!" Amber called. She ran after him—and accidentally tore her gown! How could she go to the ball now?

Sofia stood in front of her own mirror and stared at herself in her fancy gown and glittering tiara. She felt like a real princess!

For the first time that week, Sofia was actually looking forward to the ball!

King Roland proudly escorted a beaming Sofia into the ballroom.
It was time for the first waltz!
Sofia confidently spoke the magic words Cedric had given her:
"Somnibus populi cella."
Everyone instantly fell asleep—including Cedric!

"I said it wrong!" Sofia cried as she ran from the ballroom.

Sofia sank to the floor and cried. A single tear fell onto her amulet and made it glow. Suddenly, a blue light appeared—and transformed into Cinderella!

"Your amulet links all the princesses that ever were," Cinderella said. "When one of us is in trouble, another will come to help. Why are you so sad, Sofia?"

Sofia told Cinderella about trying to use a magic spell to help her become a better princess.

Cinderella smiled as she explained that she hadn't always been a princess, either. But she discovered that the people who truly cared about you didn't care which fork you used or how well you danced.

Cinderella couldn't undo the spell, but she suggested that Sofia try to become true sisters with Amber—something she'd never been able to do with her own stepsisters. "Perhaps all Amber needs is a second chance," Cinderella said. Then she disappeared!

Sofia went to Amber's room and told Amber about the spell. When Amber saw her father in the ballroom, she gasped in shock!

Sofia felt terrible. "It's all my fault," she said sadly.

Amber shook her head. "No, Sofia," she said. "You wouldn't have needed the spell if I didn't give you those trick shoes."

The girls realized that what they really needed was each other.

Together they went to Cedric's workshop to find a spell to wake everyone up. Clover, Mia, and Robin locked Cedric's pet raven, Wormwood, in his cage.

Clover tricked Wormwood into revealing where the counterspell book was hidden. Wormwood didn't realize that with her amulet, Sofia could understand every word he said.

Now Cedric's spell could be broken!

Sofia and Amber were rushing to the ballroom when Amber remembered her torn dress. "I can't go in there!" she cried.

But Sofia wasn't about to leave her sister behind. She quickly mended the gown. "Good as new!" she said.

Now it was Amber's turn to help. She led her sister in a waltz until Sofia was ready for the ball.

Sofia smiled as she took her place beside the king and read the counterspell aloud. "Populi cella excitate!" Everyone woke up.

Cedric was furious that his plan had been ruined! He flicked his wand and disappeared in a puff of smoke. "Merlin's mushrooms!" he yelled.

Meanwhile, Sofia and the king began to waltz.

Sofia looked up at her new dad. "I've been wondering. Why do they call you Roland the Second?" she asked.

"My father was also named Roland," the king explained.

"So I guess that makes me Sofia the First," Sofia said, smiling.

And it was plain to see that this princess was going to live happily ever after!

FOLLOW THAT SOUND!

Ahoy, mateys! Do you want to join my pirate crew? Then just say the pirate password, "Yo-ho-ho!" As part of my crew, you'll need to learn the Never Land pirate pledge.

TODAY'S PIRATE PLEDGE

When Never Land pirates
want something,
they ask for it nicely.

One day on Shipwreck Beach, Cubby is playing his harmonica. "Aw, coconuts! I'll never be ready in time to play at Marina's party," says Cubby sadly.

"I don't care what you say, Smee!" says Captain Hook.
"I do not need a—*yawn*—nap."

"Oh, Cap'n," says Smee, "you know how cranky you get when
you don't have your nappy-nap."

"All right, Smee," says Hook. "A little nappy might do me good."

Hook is drifting off to sleep in his hammock, when suddenly he is startled awake by the sound of music!

Why did the pirate eat candy before bedtime?

"One of those puny pirates is making an awful racket with his blowy music thing!" says Hook.

"Why don't you ask the sea pups nicely if they'll be a little quieter?" says Smee.

"Smee, who do you think you're dealing with?" says Hook.
"Why would I ask nicely when I can take the blowy thing away!"

He wanted to have sweet dreams!

SWOOSH!

"YAY-HEY, THAT'S THE WAY," says Izzy.
"You're getting better already, Cubby!"
"You'll be a harmonica master in no time," says Skully.
"Not if I can help it!" calls Captain Hook.

Hook uses his fishing hook to nab the harmonica right out of Cubby's mouth!

"My harmonica!" says Cubby.

"We gotta get it back!" says Jake.

That sneaky snook never stops fishing for trouble!

Startled, Smee throws the harmonica up in the air . . . but it doesn't come back down!

"Um, Cap'n," says Smee, "the harmonica just disappeared!"

"I don't care if it sprouted wings and flew away," says Hook, "so long as I have peace and quiet for my nap."

"**CRACKERS!**" says Skully. "That monkey took the harmonica!"
"Mr. Monkey, may I have my harmonica back, please?" asks Cubby.
"Oo-oo!" The monkey swings off toward the Never Jungle.

"I'd take that as a no," says Skully.

"He's heading for the Never Jungle," says Cubby.

"Come on, crew," says Jake. "Follow that monkey!"

Why did the monkey take the harmonica?

"But how?" asks Cubby.

"Monkey see, monkey do," says Jake.

"Great idea," says Izzy. "We can swing on the vines just like the monkey!"

"Wait for me," calls Cubby.

"Uh-oh," says Skully. "I lost sight of the monkey!"

"He could be anywhere in this jungle," says Cubby.

Just then, the crew hears music!

"It's my harmonica," says Cubby.

"Follow that sound," says Jake.

He's gone bananas!

"Hi, Mr. Monkey," says Jake. "I'm glad you like the harmonica, but it belongs to my friend Cubby."

"And I need it to practice for the big party tonight!" adds Cubby.

"OO-OO-OO," says the monkey, crossing his arms.

"He doesn't want to give the harmonica back," says Izzy.

"If only we had another instrument," says Jake.
"Then we could trade with the monkey."

"That's a great idea," says Izzy.

"But we don't have another instrument," says Cubby.

"Not yet," says Izzy. "But we can make an instrument for the monkey to play." Izzy picks up two coconuts.

"Now we need something to put inside," says Izzy.

"I found some rocks," says Cubby.

"I've got some shells," says Skully.

"How about some sand?" says Jake.

"Perfect," says Izzy.

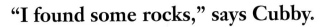
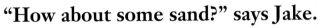
What instrument do fish like to play?

55

SHAKE-A, SHAKE-A, SHAKE-A!

"Awesome! You made maracas for the monkey," says Jake.

The eel-ectric guitar!

The monkey gives Cubby back his harmonica.

"Thanks!" says Cubby. "Hey, do you wanna come back to Shipwreck Beach and jam with me?"

"OO-oo-OO," says the happy monkey.

Cubby and the monkey play music together on the beach!
"Blast it, now there's twice as much racket!" says Captain Hook.

"What's the matter?" asks Jake.

"The Cap'n can't have his nappy-nap, what with all that music," says Smee.

"Why didn't you just ask us to be quieter?" asks Jake.

"But, how can I practice for the party?" says Cubby.

"I've got an idea," says Jake.

Cubby and the monkey play a gentle lullaby for
Captain Hook. Mr. Smee sings:

"Cap'n, close your weary eyes.
Now it's time for beddy-bye.
The music's sweet, it's not too shabby.
When you wake up, you won't be crabby."

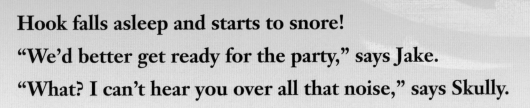

Hook falls asleep and starts to snore!

"We'd better get ready for the party," says Jake.

"What? I can't hear you over all that noise," says Skully.

Later that night, Cubby and the monkey play their instruments at Marina's party!

"Cubby, thank you so much for playing," says Marina. "You were amazing!"

"You're welcome," says Cubby, blushing.

"Yo-ho, way to go!" says Jake. "See? All that practicing paid off!"

"Can't you hear it, Smee?" asks Captain Hook.

"Hear what, Cap'n?" asks Smee.

"That blasted lullaby. I can't get it out of me head," says Hook.

"Oh, dear, you're imagining things, Cap'n," says Smee.

"I guess I am," says Hook.

"I can see why. It was a catchy tune, if I do say so myself," says Smee. "And the lyrics were top-notch."

Uh-oh! The monkey has stowed away on the *Jolly Roger!*

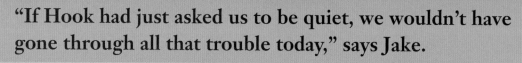

"If Hook had just asked us to be quiet, we wouldn't have gone through all that trouble today," says Jake.

"Yeah, Hook should know better! If you need something, you should ask nicely," says Izzy.

"Yeah, but if the monkey didn't take the harmonica, we never would've gotten to jam together!" says Cubby.

"Check it out! For solving pirate problems today, we earned some Gold Doubloons," says Jake.

"Let's count 'em," says Cubby.

I love a happy ending! Squawk to ya next time!

"We earned eleven Gold Doubloons," says Jake. "Yo-ho, way to go!"

Meet the Gang

Stuffy

Stuffy is a rambunctious stuffed dragon. He is brave and silly, with a tendency to run into things. His greatest wish is to be able to fly, like a real dragon! Whether Stuffy is trying to fly or is getting into trouble, he's always good for a laugh!

Doc McStuffins

Doc is six years old, and she has a secret. She has a magic stethoscope that can bring her toys to life! Doc loves helping her friends when they aren't feeling their best. She makes sure to write down each diagnosis in her Big Book of Boo-Boos.

Hallie

Hallie is Doc's lovable hippo receptionist. She keeps things running smoothly. Hallie is always ready to give Doc a helping hand, but that doesn't mean she doesn't know how to have fun!

Lambie

Lambie is Doc's stuffed lamb who just loves to cuddle! She doesn't like to get dirty and always tries to look her best. Lambie is a loyal friend and always reminds Doc that she can do anything she sets her mind to!

Chilly

Chilly is a hypochondriac stuffed snowman. He's always saying, "I hope I don't melt!" And when Doc reminds him that he's not a real snowman, Chilly fills with relief. He's a little stuffed snowman with a big personality.

Engine Nine, Feelin' Fine!

"Lambie!" calls Doc McStuffins. "It's time to open the clinic."
Doc can't find Lambie anywhere. "Has anyone seen Lambie?" she asks.
"Oops!" Doc giggles. She puts on her magic stethoscope and her toys spring to life.
"I don't know where she is!" Stuffy says.

Suddenly, Doc's brother bursts into her room, pushing his toy fire engine.
In a flash, Doc's toys go stuffed!
"Will you play firefighter with me?" Donny asks.
"Maybe later, okay?" says Doc.
Doc scoops up Lambie and Stuffy as Donny leaves.

Doc hurries out to the backyard.

"I'm going outside to play, Mom!" she calls.

"Okay, sweetie," Doc's mom says. "Just take care. It's a very hot day!"

"I will," Doc answers.

Doc McStuffins opens the door to her clinic and flips over the welcome sign. "The Doc is in!" she says.

"Hi, Hallie!" says Doc. "Do we have any toys that need fixing?"
"No patients yet," answers Hallie. "My, my. It sure is hot today."
"It's even too hot to cuddle," says Lambie.

Just then, Squeakers bounces through the door.
"Squeak, squeak, squeeeeaaak!"
"What's he saying?" Stuffy asks.
"I don't know. I don't speak squeak," says Hallie.
Doc has an idea. "Squeakers, can you show us what's wrong?"

Squeakers leads Doc and the others into the backyard.
"What's wrong with you, Engine Nine?" says Donny. "I'll give you one more chance, but that's it." He pumps Lenny's siren and points Lenny's hose at a pretend fire, but nothing comes out! "Oh, no," says Donny. "You're broken!"

Donny sets Lenny on a pile of broken toys.

"Sorry, Lenny," he says sadly. "You were an awesome toy. I'm going to miss you."

"Awww, Donny looks so sad," says Doc.

"I know how you can cheer up Donny," says Lambie.

"Fix Lenny!" Stuffy says.

As soon as Donny walks away, Doc and the others run over to Lenny.
"What's wrong, Lenny?" asks Stuffy.
"I keep running out of water," Lenny says. "A fire truck that can't put out a fire isn't much good."
"Let's get you to the clinic, Lenny," Doc says. "It's time for a checkup."

Lenny is a little nervous. "What is a checkup, anyway?" he asks.
"It's when a doctor takes a look at you to make sure you're healthy," says Lambie.
Doc listens to Lenny's heartbeat.

"Sounds perfect," she says. "Lenny, has anything been bothering you?"
"Well, I've been feeling kind of tired and my head hurts sometimes,"
Lenny admits. "Mostly on really hot days."

Just then, there's a knock at the door!
"Doc, I have something for you!" calls Doc's mom.
"Hurry," Doc says to her toys. "Go stuffed!"

"Hi, Mom," says Doc. "What's up?"

"I brought you some water, sweetie," says Doc's mom. "I don't want you to get dehydrated."

"What's dehydrated?" Doc asks.

"If you don't drink enough water, especially on a hot day, you can feel sick."

"Dehydrated," repeats Doc. "That's it! Thanks, Mom."

"I know what's wrong," announces Doc. "Lenny, you have Driedout-a-tosis!"
"Oh, my! That sounds like it should go straight into the Big Book of Boo-Boos!"
says Hallie.

"What's Driedout-a-tosis mean, Doc?" asks Lenny.
"It's like when you are dehydrated. Dehydrated is when you aren't drinking enough water," Doc explains. "Drinking water is important. But when it's hot outside, it's even more important!"

Doc puts the glass of water in front of Lenny. "Drink it all up," she says.
"Ah," says Lenny. "I feel better already!"

Hallie looks into the fire hose. "Is this thing working now?" she asks.
Squirt! "Yep, it sure as stuffin' is!" laughs Hallie.

Donny is surprised to see Doc with his fire truck.
"Engine Nine! What are you doing here?"
Lenny shoots a stream of water out of his hose.
"Awesome!" Donny shouts. "You're working again!
I missed you, buddy."

"Help! Help!" shouts Doc. "We have to rescue Stuffy from the burning building!"
"Don't worry, Stuffy," yells Donny. "Engine Nine will save you!"

Donny points Lenny's hose at the pretend fire and water gushes out!
"Whoa!" Donny says. "Great job, Engine Nine!"

"Thanks for playing with me, Doc," Donny says. "You're the best sister ever."
"I love hanging out with you, Donny," says Doc. "Almost as much as our toys do!"

Doc's Tips for Staying Healthy on a Hot, Sunny Day

- Put on sunblock to protect yourself from sunburn.

- Wear a hat to stay cool.

- Take a break from the sun! Rest in the shade or inside.

- Tell an adult if you feel dizzy or have a headache.

- Drink lots of water all day long. That way you won't get dehydrated.

Blooming Bows

It's a busy day at Minnie's Bow-tique.
Minnie and Daisy are getting ready for two
special visitors.
"Daisy," says Minnie, "did you find the camera?"

"Not yet," replies Daisy.
"But I know I have it here somewhere!"

Daisy turns around. "Here it is, Daisy," says Minnie. "Thanks!" says Daisy. "Now I'll be able to get a good picture of you and the twins."

Just then, Minnie hears giggling.
"Get ready!" she cries. "Here they come!"

"Ta-daaah!" Millie and Melody shout.

"I'm Purple Posy!" says Melody.
"And I'm Rosie Posy!" says Millie.

Minnie greets her twin nieces while Daisy snaps a picture of them.

"Hold that pose, pretty posies!" cries Daisy.

"Oh!" says Minnie. "You both look simply adorable!"

As the girls twirl around to show off their costumes,
some of the flower petals fall off.

Daisy snaps away as Cuckoo-Loca flies in for a closer look.

"All set for the Posy Pageant?" asks Cuckoo-Loca.

"We sure are, Cuckoo-Loca!" says Millie. "Come on, Melody, let's show them our posy prance dance!"

As the girls dance, more and more paper petals fall to the floor.

"Is that supposed to happen?" whispers Cuckoo-Loca, pointing to all the petals on the floor.

The girls sing:
"We can dance! We can sing!
On the first day of spring!
But you better make room,
'Cause it's time to bloom!"

"Oh, my," Minnie says.
"That bloom went *ka-boom!*" adds Cuckoo-Loca.

The twins stare at all the petals on the floor.
"Uh-oh," says Melody. "I guess the glue wasn't dry."
"I'll say," says Cuckoo-Loca.

"Don't worry, girls," Minnie says. "We'll fix these right up."
"Oh, please hurry, Aunt Minnie!" says Melody.
"Or else we can't be in the pageant!" cries Millie.

"I've got the sticky-wicky goo-glue!" Daisy cries.
"Good thinking, Daisy!" says Minnie.

Minnie watches as Daisy glues the petals back on. "Let's see, this pink one goes here, this purple one goes there . . . wait . . . is that right?" asks Daisy.

"Daisy!" says Melody. "I'm Purple Posy! She's Rosie Posy!"

Minnie gives the twins a big hug. "There, there, now, girls," she says. "I'll figure something out."

"But how?" asks Melody. "It's a flower show, not a *bow* show!"

Suddenly, Minnie has an idea. "Girls!" she calls. "Follow me!" Grabbing an armful of fabric, Minnie leads the girls to the dressing room.

While Minnie cuts fabric and ties ribbons, the twins giggle excitedly. Daisy and Cuckoo-Loca can't wait to see what Minnie is creating.

Soon, Minnie reappears.
"Ladies and gentle-bird, introducing our
favorite flowers: Rosie Posy and Purple Posy!"

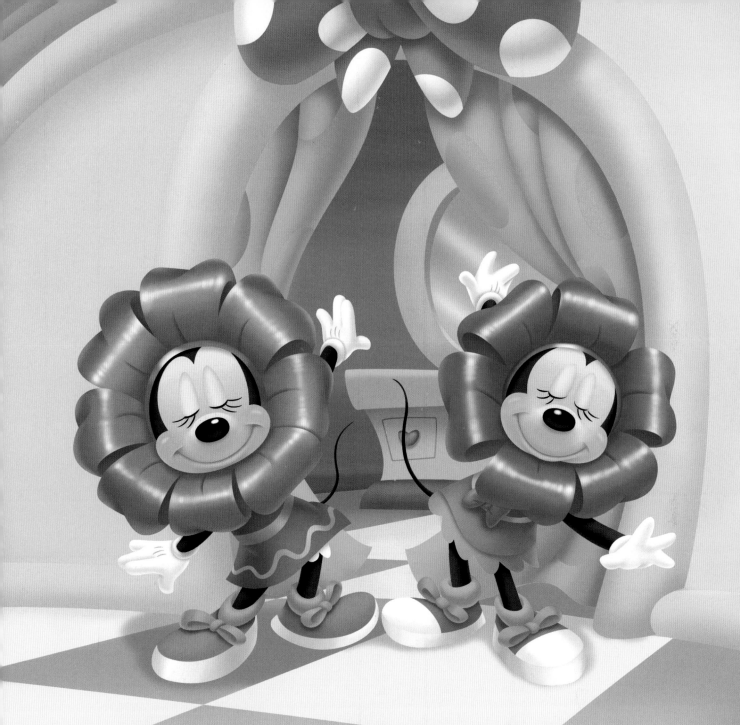

"Pop-up posies!" cries Daisy. "And no glue needed!"
"Now that's what I call getting out of a sticky situation,"
says Cuckoo-Loca.

Minnie gathers the twins. "Come on, my little posies. It's showtime!"

"Hey, girls!" Daisy calls, holding up her camera.
"Say *posies*!"

125

Millie and Melody wave good-bye as they run out the door.

"Wow, Minnie!" says Daisy, smiling at her friend.
"Who knew you had such flower power?"

"It's like I always say, Daisy," says Minnie.
"There's no business like *bow* business!"

The Royal
Slumber Party

Sofia and Amber are having a royal sleepover tonight!

"This is where we'll be sleeping," Amber says.

"The observatory? We get to sleep under the stars!" Sofia cries.

"It's a royal slumber party," Amber says. "Everything has to be amazing."

Sofia's two best friends, Ruby and Jade, are coming!

Amber is shocked. "You invited village girls? You're a princess now. You should only invite princesses to royal parties!"

"But Ruby and Jade are fun!" Sofia assures Amber. "You'll see."

The royal herald's trumpet sounds. "They're here!" Sofia cries.
Amber's friends, Princess Hildegard and Princess Clio, step out
of their coaches. Behind them are Jade and Ruby in an oxcart.
"I can't believe we're here!" Jade exclaims, hugging Sofia.
"We're so excited!" Ruby adds.

It's time for the party to start! The princesses change into
fancy nightgowns. Ruby and Jade giggle as they roll their hair
in pinecone curlers—just like at home.

"We're at a royal sleepover!" they chant, pulling Sofia up to
join their silly dance.

The other princesses stare at Ruby and Jade.

"What are they wearing?" Hildegard says.

"What are they doing?" Clio wonders.

Amber frowns. "Are those pinecones?"

Ruby hears her and dances over. "Want one? We brought extras."

Amber marches over to Sofia. "Sofia! Pinecones
are not part of a perfect princess slumber party."
Sofia's worried. She wants her new sister and her
old friends to like each other.
"They can fit in," she says. "They just need a little help."

Sofia has a great idea. "How would you two like a royal makeover?" she asks her friends.

Ruby and Jade squeal with excitement!

Baileywick and Sofia's woodland friends help out. They fix the girls' hair and dress them in pretty gowns and tiaras.

Sofia makes her friends cover their eyes. Then she leads them to a mirror. "Open your eyes," she says.

Jade and Ruby gasp when they see themselves.

"I'm a princess!" Ruby exclaims.

"Me, too!" calls Jade.

Next it's time for party activities.
First comes fan decorating.

Ruby and Jade have fun. But their
fans don't look very princessy.

Then the girls play a game of Pin the Tail
on the Unicorn. "Ooh! Ooh!" Jade says.
"Can I go first?"

But Jade ends up nowhere
near the unicorn!

After that, the girls watch Cedric, the royal sorcerer, put on a magic puppet show in the banquet hall. During the show, James, Sofia's brother, walks in with a message for the girls.

"Prince James!" Jade and Ruby squeal, rushing toward him. They're thrilled to see the friendly prince!

Jade and Ruby are so excited they accidentally knock over the chocolate milk fountain. Oops! Chocolate milk splashes onto Amber's nightgown. She is furious!

"We're so, so, so sorry!" Ruby says to Amber.

"So sorry," Jade adds.

Amber walks off in a huff while Sofia shakes her head sadly.

Baileywick hurries Jade and Ruby away to get cleaned up.
Then James tells the girls it's time for dancing in the throne room.
"Let's go," Amber says. "Maybe we can enjoy five minutes of our
party without Sofia's friends making a mess."

Now Sofia's even more worried! She goes off to find her friends.

"I want you both to fit in with the princesses," Sofia explains.

"We look just like them now, don't we?" Jade says.

"Yes," Sofia says. "But princesses don't talk so much, or laugh so loud, or make so many messes."

Jade frowns. "We were just having fun."

"We're sorry," Ruby adds quickly. "We'll try to act more like Amber and the other princesses."

"Thank you!" Sofia is relieved. Now she's sure everyone will get along!

Sofia and her friends join the others in the throne room. But Ruby and Jade don't know how to waltz. All they can do is stand there and watch the princesses dance. After a while, they tell Sofia that they want to go home.

"But you're finally fitting in!" Sofia cries. "And you're not embarrassing me anymore!"

"I'm sorry if we talk too much and laugh too loudly for your fancy new friends," says Jade. "Maybe we shouldn't be friends anymore!"

Ruby takes Jade's arm and together they rush out of the room.

"Don't worry about them," Hildegard tells Sofia. "You're with us now."

Sofia goes after her friends, but finds her mother instead.
"I was trying to help Jade and Ruby fit in," she explains.
"But I just made them feel bad."

"A true princess treats people with kindness, Sofia," Queen
Miranda says gently. "If someone is your friend, you should
like them for who they are."

Sofia knows her mother is right. She runs outside and finds her friends just as they are about to leave.

"I'm sorry about the way I acted," she says. "Please let me make it up to you. We can have our own slumber party—just the three of us!"

Jade and Ruby think for a moment and finally agree to stay.

Soon Sofia and her friends are in her room, having a great time. They laugh—loudly. They talk—a lot. They roll pinecones in their hair and perch tiaras on top.

Meanwhile, Amber and her friends go back to the observatory.

"Finally, it's just us princesses," Amber says.

"This is a perfect party," Hildegard agrees with a yawn.

There's a long silence. The princesses are really bored.

"You know," Clio speaks up, "Sofia's friends were kind of fun."

A moment later, Amber and her friends knock on Sofia's door.
"Um, do you have room for a few more princesses?" asks Amber.
Sofia looks at Jade and Ruby. "What do you think?"
"The more, the merrier," Ruby says with a smile.
Sofia and Amber end up having the perfect sleepover with
friends—old and new!

Sofia the First

Princess Lesson

A true princess
treats people with kindness.

Save Me, Smee!

Ahoy, mateys! Do you want to join my pirate crew? Then just say the pirate password, "Yo-ho-ho!" As part of my crew, you'll need to learn the Never Land pirate pledge.

TODAY'S PIRATE PLEDGE

A pirate is always willing to help out a friend.

"**B**last it, Smee! I didn't sleep a wink all night," says Hook. "Captain Cuddly is missing! You know I can't go beddy-bye without my teddy bear."

Just then, Hook spots a teeny, tiny treasure chest.

"Why, it's me first treasure chest from when I was just a wee little pirate."

There's a treasure map inside the chest!

"We have to go across Slippery Snake River through Crumble Canyon. Then X marks the spot at—gulp!—Skull Rock," says Smee. "Those are the most perilous places in all of Never Land."

"So what?" says Hook. "There's treasure and I want it."

"Be careful, Mr. Smee," says Jake. "You're heading for Slippery Snake River!"

Smee nods. "I'm afraid the Captain's after treasure."

"We could follow in case there's any trouble," says Izzy.

"Oh, you sea pups are so kind," says Smee.

Trouble is Captain Hook's middle name!

"Danger, schmanger," says Hook. "It's just a river."
Hook jumps on the back of a slippery snake.
BOING, BOING, SPLASH!
"Save me, Smee!" calls the Captain.
"Oh dear, oh dear! Right away, Cap'n!"

BOING, BOING, SPLASH! Smee falls into the river, too!

"We have to help Hook and Smee," says Jake.

"But how can we get to them?" asks Cubby. "The snakes are too slippery to jump across!"

What did the snake say when he learned to ride a bike?

"We'd better think of something quick," says Jake.

Izzy makes a lasso and tosses it to Smee. "Mr. Smee, catch!" she calls.

Then Jake and the crew pull Smee and Hook to shore.

"Great work, Iz," says Jake.

"Thank you, sea pups," whispers Smee.

"See? That wasn't dangerous at all," says Hook as he staggers to the shore and falls down.

"Oh, my," says Smee. "What do you say we go back to the *Jolly Roger* now, Cap'n? I'll make you a nice cup of tea."

"Never!" says Hook. "Crumble Canyon awaits!"

Look, Ma, no hands!

"**CRACKERS!** Hook and Smee are going across that narrow pass," says Skully.

"Be ready to lend a hand, crew," says Jake.

"See, Smee? This is a breeze," says Captain Hook.
"I don't even know why they call it Crumble Canyon."

"Well, sir," says Smee, "it's because the sides of the canyon tend to . . ."

"AIIEEEE!" yells Hook as the ground beneath him collapses.

" . . . crumble," finishes Smee.

"Save me, Smee!" yells Hook.

"I gotcha, Cap'n," says Smee.

"But who has *you*?" asks Hook.

"Ahh!" Smee starts to fall over the edge of the canyon.

Skully swoops in and grabs Smee.

"I got you, Skully," calls Cubby.

"And I've got *you*," says Izzy.

"Come on, crew! Heave ho! Heave ho!" calls Jake.

Together, they hoist Hook and Smee to safety.

"Are you . . . okay . . . sir?" Smee pants.

"I'll be better when I have that treasure," says Hook.

"Are you sure you don't want to go home? I'll make hot chocolate with those little marshmallows you like so much."

"I do love little marshmallows," says Hook, "but Skull Rock and treasure await!"

"Hook can't go to Skull Rock," says Cubby. "It's way too dangerous."

"He'll never give up looking for that treasure," says Smee.

"Unless," says Izzy, "there was an even *better* treasure for him to find."

What do you call a pirate who lives in the mountains?

"Great idea, Iz," says Jake. "We can make a new treasure for Hook to find. Somewhere nice and safe."

"But we don't have any treasure," says Cubby.

"I know where there's a treasure that the Cap'n will just love," says Smee.

"Skully, send word to Sharky and Bones to prepare the treasure," says Jake.
"AYE-AYE!" Skully says.

"Cubby, can you make a new map?" Jake asks.
"AYE-AYE, JAKE!" says Cubby.

Lost!

"Now to get Hook to take the bait," says Jake. "Hey, Izzy," he says loudly enough for Hook to hear. "I can't believe we found a map to the most awesome treasure in all of Never Land!"

"Yeah. Lucky Captain Hook isn't around to take our map to the really awesome treasure," says Izzy.

"Ha! You can't fool the great Captain Hook. I'll be taking the map *and* the treasure," says Hook.

"AW, COCONUTS," says Cubby, winking at Smee. "You tricked us again."

"We'll never find the awesome treasure now," says Skully.

"I don't believe me eyes," says Hook. "The treasure is aboard the *Jolly Roger!*"

"Oh, is that so?" asks Smee innocently.

"The most awesome treasure in all of Never Land—right on me own ship," says Hook happily.

"Look alive," says Hook. "There be treasure aboard."

"X marks the spot," says Smee.

It's Captain Cuddly!

"Oh, my little cuddly wuddly! You are the greatest treasure in all of Never Land. Yes, you are," says Hook.

All this baby talk is making me sicky wicky! Blech!

"He had a little rip," says Bones, "but I fixed him right up."

"Did you have an ouchy, Captain Cuddly?" asks Hook.

"Whew!" says Smee. "Now that we're home, I imagine you won't be needing any more rescuing today, Cap'n."

"Rescuing? What do you mean rescuing?" says Hook. "The great Captain Hook has never needed to be rescued. Isn't that right, Captain Cuddly?"

SPLASH! Hook accidentally knocks his bear overboard.

"Bear overboard!" yells Hook. He dives into the water . . . and finds his bear in the arms of the Tick Tock Croc!

"Save me, Smee! And Captain Cuddly, too!"

"Right away, Cap'n," Smee says as he jumps into the water.

Meet the Gang

Stuffy

Stuffy is a rambunctious stuffed dragon. He is brave and silly, with a tendency to run into things. His greatest wish is to be able to fly, like a real dragon! Whether Stuffy is trying to fly or is getting into trouble, he's always good for a laugh!

Doc McStuffins

Doc is six years old, and she has a secret. She has a magic stethoscope that can bring her toys to life! Doc loves helping her friends when they aren't feeling their best. She makes sure to write down each diagnosis in her Big Book of Boo-Boos.

Hallie

Hallie is Doc's lovable hippo receptionist. She keeps things running smoothly. Hallie is always ready to give Doc a helping hand, but that doesn't mean she doesn't know how to have fun!

Lambie

Lambie is Doc's stuffed lamb who just loves to cuddle! She doesn't like to get dirty and always tries to look her best. Lambie is a loyal friend and always reminds Doc that she can do anything she sets her mind to!

Chilly

Chilly is a hypochondriac stuffed snowman. He's always saying, "I hope I don't melt!" And when Doc reminds him that he's not a real snowman, Chilly fills with relief. He's a little stuffed snowman with a big personality.

Bubble Trouble

Doc likes to play with her best friend, Emmie, and Emmie's little sister, Alma. One of their favorite toys is a Bubble Monkey bubble blower.

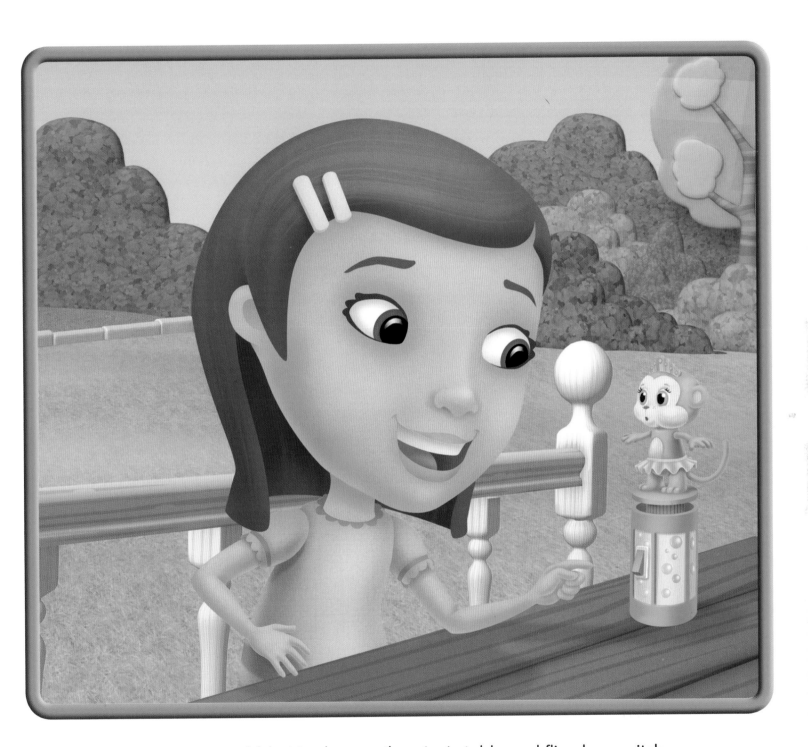

Emmie puts Bubble Monkey on the picnic table and flips her switch.
Three…two…one…

Bubbles, bubbles everywhere!
Alma pops three bubbles, and Emmie pops six.
Doc pops two bubbles at once!

Emmie's dog, Rudi, wants to pop bubbles, too.
But Bubble Monkey isn't working anymore. She's all out of bubbles.

Alma fills up Bubble Monkey while Doc and Emmie chase after Rudi.
When she's done, she asks, "Is everyone ready?"
They are!

Three…two…one…
But no bubbles!

"Where are the bubbles?" asks Alma.
"I'll take a look and see if I can figure out what's wrong," says Doc.

Doc takes Bubble Monkey to her clinic and brings her to life
with her magic stethoscope.
"Hey, look!" Stuffy says. "Doc brought Bubble Monkey over to play."

"Sorry, Stuffy, but Bubble Monkey is here for a checkup," says Doc.

First, Doc runs some tests. She takes a feather from her bag.
She asks Bubble Monkey to blow it.
Bubble Monkey blows, but the feather barely moves.

"Let the dragon try it!" says Stuffy.
Stuffy blows the feather right out of Doc's hand!
It lands on Chilly's face.
"Achoo!" Chilly sneezes.

Next, Doc listens to Bubble Monkey's chest.
"Sounds like goop is blocking your bubble pumper," she says.
"Are you having any other symptoms?"
"What are symptoms?" asks Bubble Monkey.

Doc explains that symptoms are things that hurt.
"It's your body's way of telling you that something is wrong."
"Well, I have a tummy ache," Bubble Monkey says.

"Can I give your tummy a little squeeze?" Doc asks.
She presses Bubble Monkey's stomach.
Something shoots out and hits Stuffy in the chest. "Ick!" says Stuffy.

Now Stuffy and Chilly are stuck together!
"Weird," says Doc as she pulls them apart. "This is paste."

Doc heads back to Emmie's yard to investigate.
"Alma, what did you put in Bubble Monkey?" she asks.

Alma holds up the pink jar. "I used this," she says.
"Alma, the pink one is paste!" Emmie says.
"The green one is the bubble soap!"

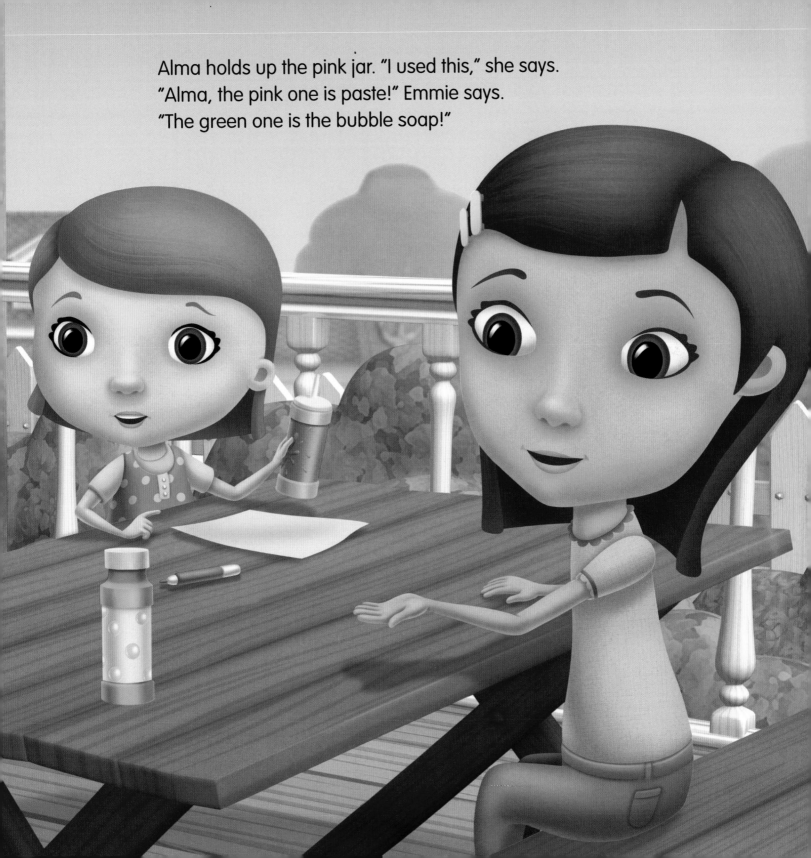

Doc rushes back to the clinic.
"I have a diagnosis!" she tells Bubble Monkey.
"You have a bad case of Gunk-inside-atude."

"Toys need to get filled right, just like people need to eat right," says Doc.
Then Doc cleans out Bubble Monkey's tubes and fills her up with bubble soap.

"Thanks, Doc. I feel better!" says Bubble Monkey.
"You're super fantastic!"

"I love my job!" says Doc.
"Now let's get you back to Emmie and Alma."

"I'm back!" Doc says.
"And this time, I brought Bubble Monkey!"

"Did you fix her?" Alma asks.
"There's only one way to find out," says Doc.
Three...two...one...

Bubbles!

Doc's Tips on Eating Right

• We have to eat the right things to make our bodies healthy and feel good.

• Eat a good breakfast each morning.

• Cut down on sweets and candy.

• Eat plenty of healthy fruits and vegetables.

• Try to stay away from fried, fatty foods.

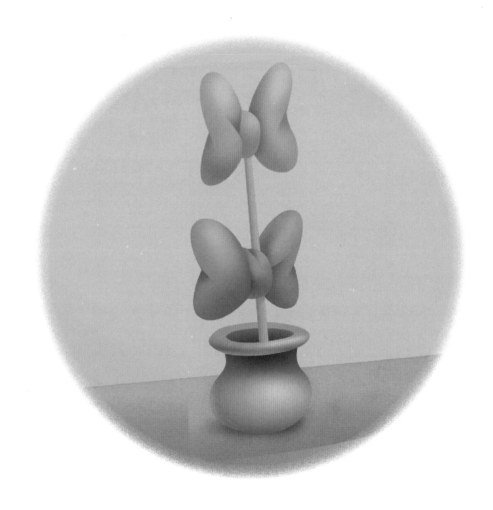

Disney MINNIE

Trouble Times Two

Minnie is hard at work in her busy Bow-tique. "Oh, Cuckoo-Loca," says Minnie, "isn't my new magic bejeweler fantastic?"

Suddenly, Minnie hears giggling!
"Who's making that noise?" she says.
"It's us, Aunt Minnie!" shout Millie
and Melody, popping out at her.

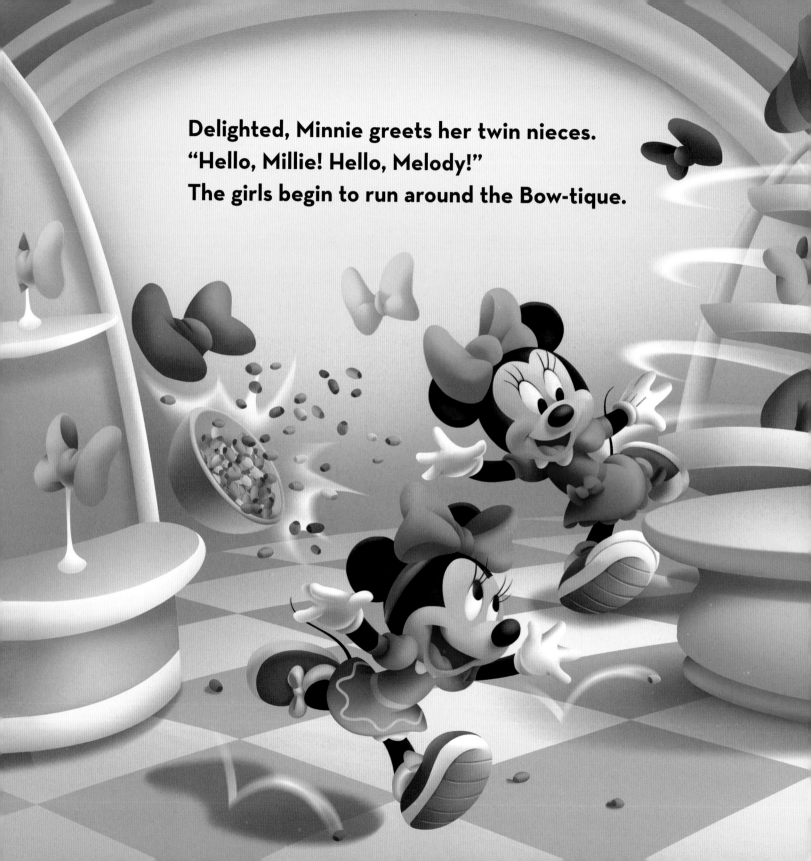

Delighted, Minnie greets her twin nieces.
"Hello, Millie! Hello, Melody!"
The girls begin to run around the Bow-tique.

Oh, no! They accidentally knock over boxes of bows and beads!

"Can we help you make stuff today?" Millie asks.
"We promise to be extra good," adds Melody.
"I was just thinking how nice it would be to have
two helpers today," says Minnie.
"Yay!" shout Millie and Melody.

Just then, Daisy Duck rushes into the shop. "Minnie!" she calls excitedly. "You're never going to believe it . . . ."

Oops-a-*Daisy!* She slips on the spilled beads and falls!

"Oh, Daisy!" cries Minnie. "Are you all right?"

"Never better," says Daisy. "Guess what famous movie superstar is on her way over to the Bow-tique right now?"
"Penelope Poodle?" guesses Minnie.
"Right!" cries Daisy. "I just got off the phone with her people. They made me promise that Penelope could shop in total peace and quiet."

Suddenly, Millie and Melody zoom past Daisy, nearly knocking her over.
"Hi, Daisy," the twins shout. "Sorry about the beads!"

Daisy looks at the girls and sighs. "Minnie, the twins are *not* total peace and quiet."

"Normally that's true," says Minnie. "But they promised to be extra good today."

Just then, the glamorous Penelope Poodle
glides through the door.
"Welcome to my Bow-tique," says Minnie.

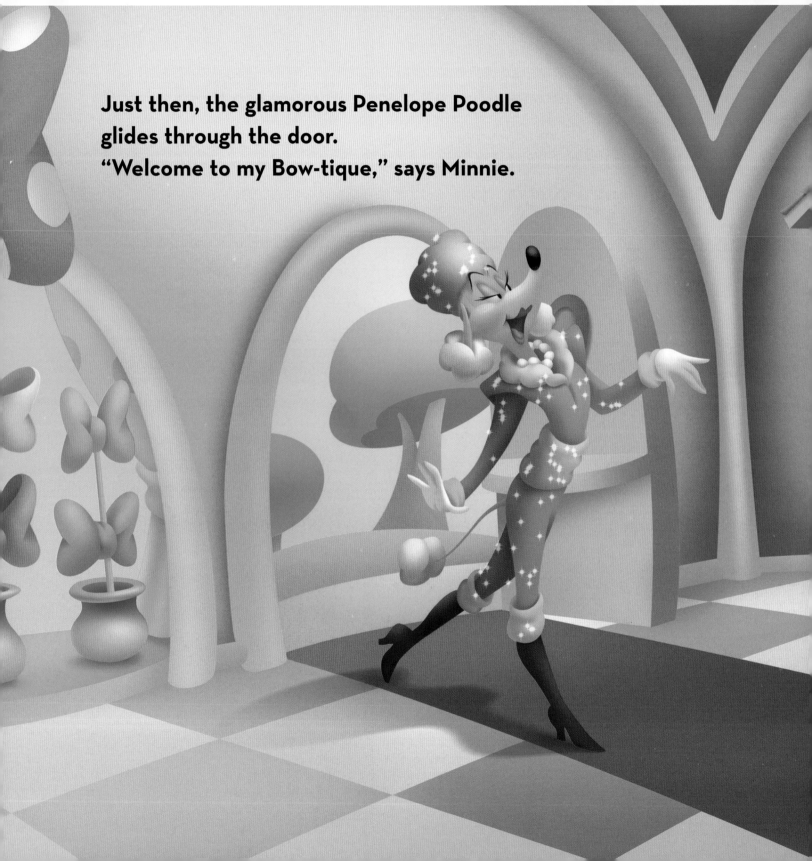

"Hello," says Penelope. "You must help me. I'm accepting a Golden Bone award in less than an hour, and I need something fabulous to wear!"

Suddenly, Millie and Melody race past Penelope!
"Beep, beep!" shouts Millie.
"Coming through!" warns Melody.

Penelope Poodle gasps. "I was promised I could shop in total peace and quiet."

Thinking fast, Minnie picks up the sparkly bow she made with her magic bejeweler and shows it to Penelope. "I call it the Glitterati," says Minnie. Penelope Poodle is very impressed.

Suddenly, Millie and Melody crash into
some of Minnie's bow displays!
"Look out!" shout the twins.

They knock over racks of bows, ribbons, and even a can of paint. The paint splatters everywhere!

Penelope Poodle has had enough. "I can see that coming here was a mistake."

"I am positive I can find you something gorgeous to wear," Minnie says, "if you'll just wait."

"Wait?" says Penelope. "I can't waste another moment!
I simply must go!"

"What have those little monsters done to me?"

"Oh, they're not little monsters," says Minnie.
"They're little helpers!"
She quickly adds bows and jewels to the twins'
handiwork. "I think they're on to something!"

Penelope Poodle looks in the mirror.
"I look fabulous!" she says. "You're brilliant!"
Minnie smiles sweetly.
"That's what I always say," Daisy agrees.

Everyone loves Penelope's new outfit.
"Miss Poodle!" calls a fan. "That's a fantastic look!"
"Who are you wearing?" asks a photographer.
Penelope smiles. "Who else? Minnie Mouse, of course!"

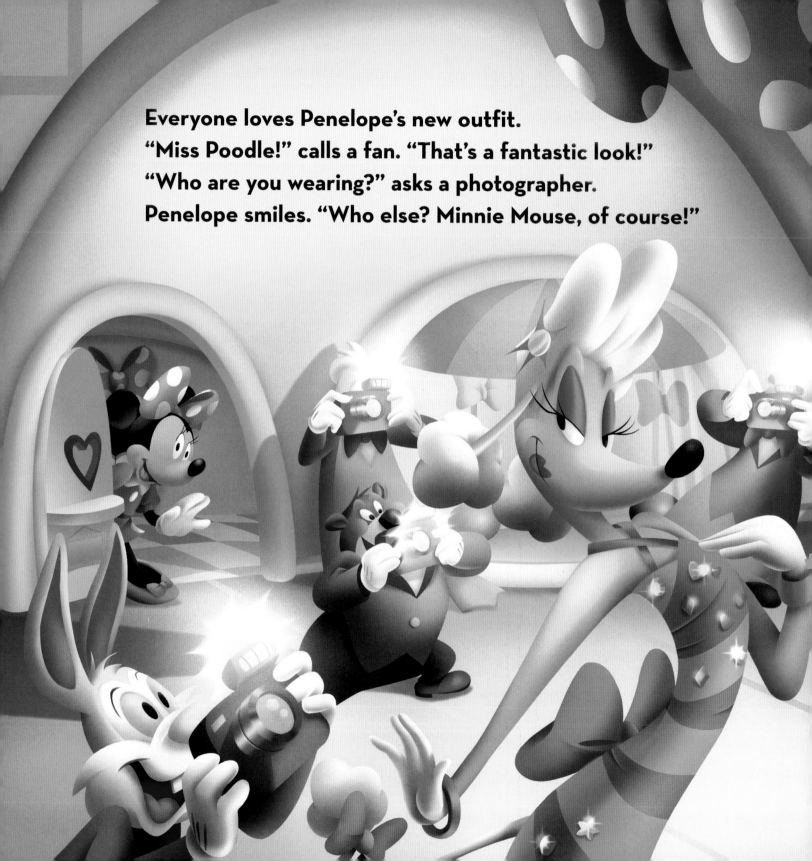

Millie and Melody look at the mess they made
in the Bow-tique.
"We'll clean up for you, Aunt Minnie," they promise.

Daisy lets out a sigh of relief. "I don't know how you do it," she says, shaking her head.

"Oh, Daisy," says Minnie, "I'm just trying to spread happiness, one bow at a time."

LET'S GET JUMPING!

Ahoy, mateys! Do you want to join my pirate crew? Then just say the pirate password, "Yo-ho-ho!" As part of my crew, you'll need to learn the Never Land pirate pledge.

TODAY'S PIRATE PLEDGE

Being a brave pirate means knowing when to ask for help from your mateys.

ne day, Jake and his crew are playing on the beach.
Suddenly, Skully notices something. "Package, ahoy!"
"Maybe it's treasure," says Cubby.
"Only one way to find out," says Jake. "Let's open 'er up!"

"Yo-ho, way to go!" says Jake. "It's a pogo stick!"

"What are we waiting for? Let's get jumping," says Izzy.
BOING, BOING! The crew takes turns jumping.
"Coconuts!" says Cubby, losing his balance. "This pogo
stick is awfully springy!"

"Don't worry, Cubby," says Jake. "You just need some practice."
"I'll try again later," says Cubby.

What goes "boing—arrgh—boing—arrgh"?

"Smee, will you hold still?" says Captain Hook.

"Sorry, Cap'n, it's just that this wind is so . . . windy," says Smee.

"How am I ever going to get me hat down from that blasted tree?" Hook wonders aloud.

Just then, they hear . . . BOING, BOING, BOING!

"Did you see that?" asks Hook. "That puny pirate used that sproingy thing to get a banana out of a tree!"

"That's nice, but I'm not ready for a snack," says Smee.

"No, you **SCURVY SEA DOG!** If I had that bouncy thing, I could get me hat!" says Hook.

Why, a pirate on a pogo stick, of course!

"WHOA!" says Cubby.

"Steady as she goes," says Jake. "You're doing great!"

YOINK! Hook uses his plunger hook to grab the pogo stick!

"Yay-hey, no way!" calls Izzy.

"That sneaky snook took our pogo stick," says Cubby.

The crew's pogoing has turned into no-going!

BOING! "Look, Smee!" calls Hook. "I got me hat!"

"That's good, sir," calls Smee. "Now you better stop before you hurt yourself."

"Nonsense," says Hook. "How could I possibly—ouch!"

"Smee! This blasted thing is broken," yells Hook.

"Cap'n, where are you going?" calls Smee.

"To get me hat!" calls Hook.

Sharky and Bones sing as the captain bounces by.

"Oh, the captain he was slick,
And he nabbed a pogo stick.
A stolen stick? Why, that's a no-no.
Now he can't stop—he's bound to pogo
On his boingy, sproingy, youchy, ouchy, loco pogo stick!"

BOING,

BOING,

"Where could Captain Hook be?" Cubby wonders aloud.
Just then the crew hears . . .

BOING, BOING, BOING!

"I hear Hook, but I don't see him anywhere," says Izzy.

"Look!" says Jake. "Pogo-stick tracks. If we follow them, I bet we'll find Captain Hook!"

"And our pogo stick," says Skully.

BOING, BOING!

"**AIEEEEEE!**" cries Captain Hook.

"Cap'n? Cap'n, where'd you go?" says Smee.

"Up here!" shouts Hook.

"I'll throw down the sproingy, boingy thing, and you jump up here and get me," says Hook.

BOING! Smee bounces up, but he can't reach! "Smee," shouts Captain Hook, "can't you do anything right?"

"There's Mr. Smee," says Izzy.

"And our pogo stick!" says Skully.

"Thank goodness you sea pups are here," says Smee.
"Here's your pogo stick. Sorry for all the trouble."

"That's okay, Mr. Smee," says Jake. "Thanks for returning our pogo stick."

"Um, there's just one little problem," says Smee. "I'm afraid the Cap'n is, well . . . up a tree."

"CRACKERS!" says Skully. "A pirate in a tree? Now I've seen everything."

How did Hook feel when they took the pogo stick?

"Can you help him get down?" asks Smee.

"I don't need their help!" cries Hook. "I can get down on my . . . WHOOOOAAAAAAAA!"

"Oh, no," says Cubby. "He's going to fall!"

"We have to help him—and fast," says Jake.

"I know what will help Captain Hook get out of that tree," says Izzy. "Pixie dust!"

"Come on, Mr. Smee," says Jake.

Izzy sprinkles everyone with pixie dust!

"Oh, my, I can fly!" says Smee.

He was hopping mad!

"I don't need help," says Hook. "I'm fi—ahhh!"
Izzy sprinkles Hook with pixie dust just in time!
"Did I crash?" asks Hook.
"No, sir," says Smee. "Look!"

"I'M FLYING!" says Hook.

"Time to fly back to Pirate Island!" says Jake.

"Thanks for your help, sea pups," says Smee.
"Now let's find your hat, Cap'n."

253

What did the ocean say to the flying pirate?

"What do you say, Cubby? Ready to give that pogo stick another try?" asks Izzy.

"I guess," says Cubby. He gets on and takes a few hops.

BOING, BOING, BOING!

"Woo-hoo! Look at me! I'm a pogo master!" calls Cubby.

"I knew you'd get the hang of it if you tried," says Jake.

Nothing. It just waved.

"Now that I have my hat back, I'm as handsome as ever," says Captain Hook.

"Oh, yes, Cap'n, you're a looker, you are," says Smee.

Wooooossssshhhhhhh!

A gust of wind blows Hook's hat right off his head!

"Barnacles! Not again," says Hook. "Catch that hat!"

"Aye, aye, Cap'n," says Smee. "Oh, look, sir, here it is, right on top of the water."

Smee is about to grab the hat when he hears . . .

"Mr. Crocodile," says Smee, "may I have that hat back . . . please?"

SNAP! The croc snaps his teeth.

Tick, Tock

"On second thought, you know, that hat looks really good on you," says Smee. "Don't you think so, Cap'n?"

"Oh, yes, very fashionable," says Hook. "N-n-now be a g-g-good crocodile and swim away!"

BACK ON PIRATE ISLAND . . .

"You know," says Jake, "if Hook had just asked for help in the first place, he wouldn't have gotten into all that trouble."

"And we wouldn't have lost our pogo stick," says Skully.

"Check it out!" says Jake. "For solving pirate problems today, we earned some Gold Doubloons!"

"Let's open the team treasure chest and count 'em," says Cubby.

And now for my final joke! What do pirates pay for corn?

"Way to go, mateys!" says Jake. "We earned eight Gold Doubloons!"

"I did it!" calls Cubby. "Whee!"

BOING, BOING, BOING!

A buck-an-ear! Ha-ha! I am too funny! See ya next time, mateys!

Minnie's Rainbow

Minnie has just finished reading a book.
She's asked all her friends to come take a look.

Read About
Rainbows

She learned about something you see in the sky,
A colorful arc that the birds fly right by.

But what makes a rainbow that follows the rain?
Let's find out as Minnie and her friends explain.

Red makes a rainbow so fiery bright.
It's for strawberries, stop signs, and Mickey's night-light.

Can you find a rainbow near Mickey's bed?
If you do, then you'll see its first color is red!

A rainbow has orange. It's cheerful and cute—
The color of tigers and sunsets and fruit.

Now look for the rainbow on the back of Goofy's car.
Then check out the color of its second bar.

Yellow gives rainbows their light, happy rays,
A reminder of ducklings and warm, sunny days.

If you spy the small rainbow that's on Pluto's bow,
You'll find the third color is one that you know!

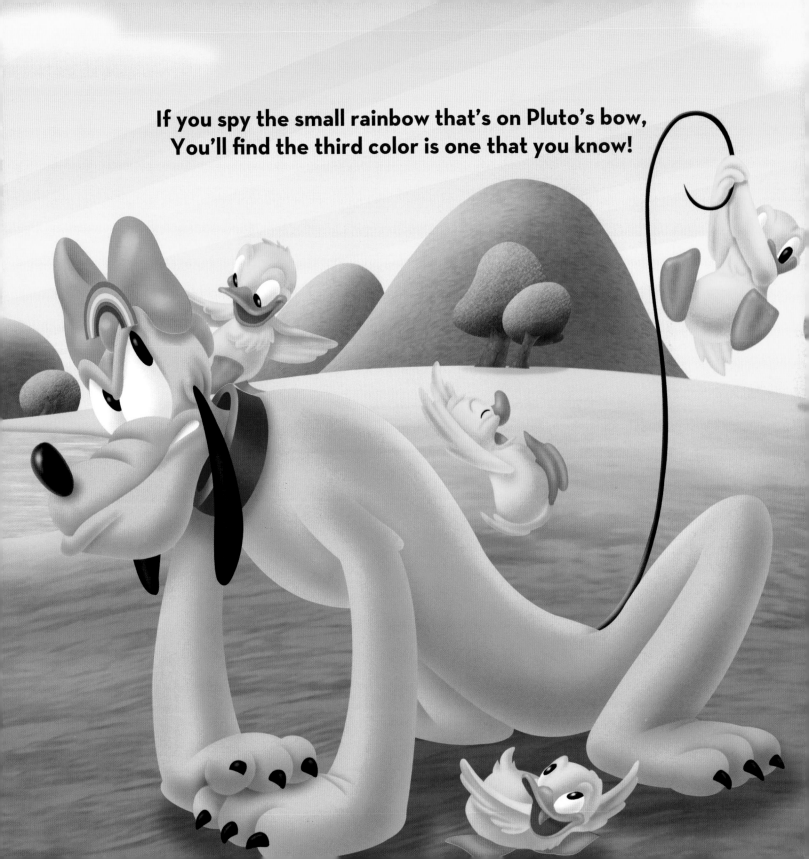

There's a garden of green in each rainbow you see.
It's for pickles and peas and the leaves of a tree.

So search for the rainbow that's next to the beans,
Then name the fourth color. That's right, it is green!

Inside every rainbow is cool, calming blue,
For blue skies and bluebells and blue dungarees, too.

Now hunt for a rainbow beside Donald's hand.
It's clear now that blue is the rainbow's fifth band.

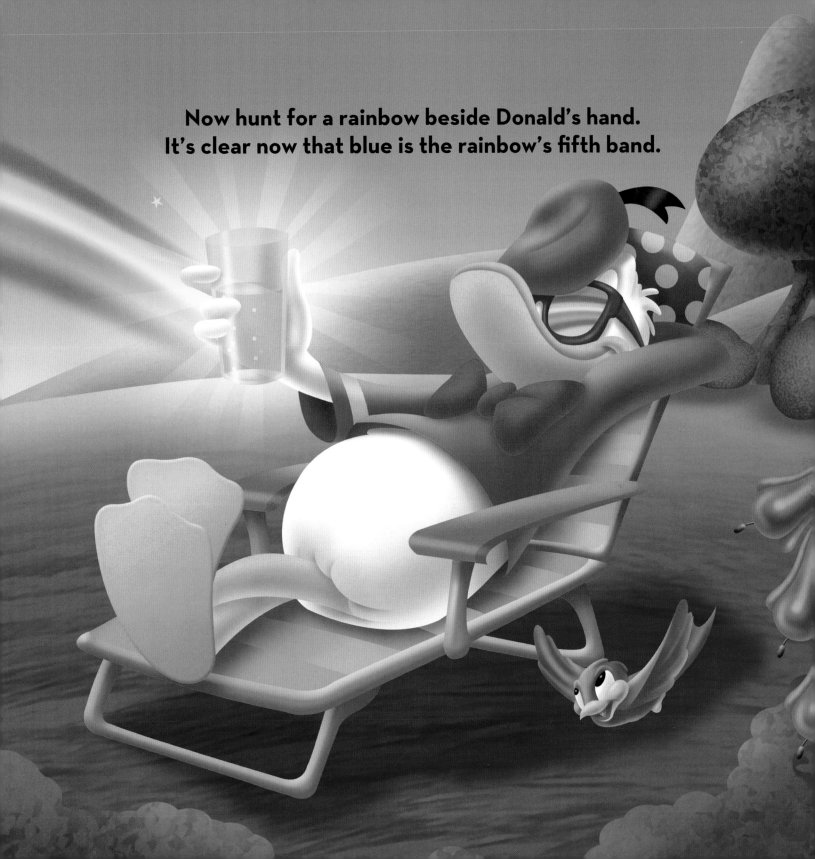

Violet you'll find at the end of the line.
It's the color of lilacs and grapes on a vine.

There's a rainbow hiding under Daisy's beak,
And violet's the sixth of its colorful streaks.

**Red, orange, and yellow are one, two, and three.
Green is four. Blue is five. Violet's six, as you can see.**

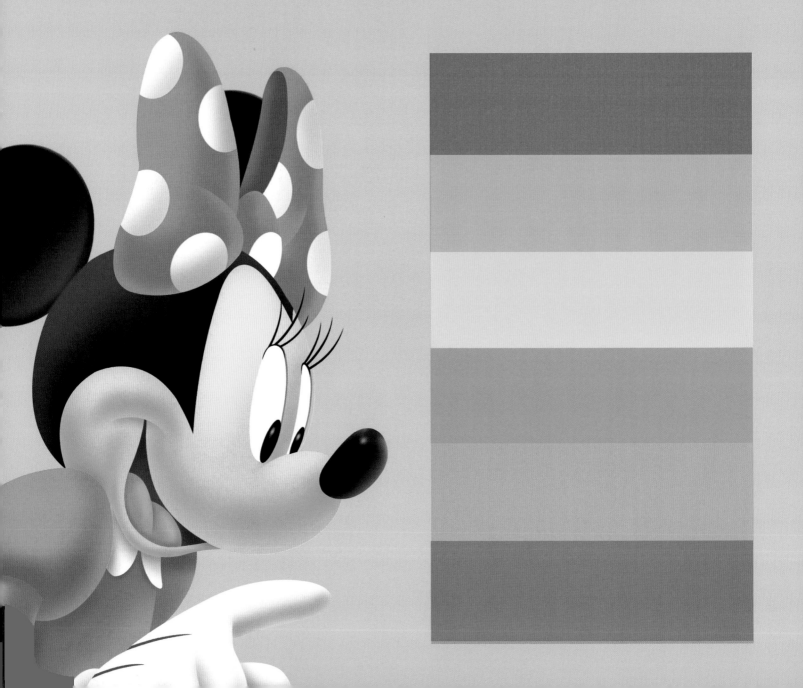

But there's more to each rainbow you see in the sky.
A whole spectrum of colors, so let's find out why!

A rainbow is made of the colors of light.
When we look at it whole, we can see only white.

But when white light is split, then more colors appear.
If you tried counting them, it might take a whole year!

There are not only colors like red, green, and blue.
There are some you can't see with your eyes. Yes, it's true!

So what makes a rainbow? What is it we see?
All the waves that are part of the light, naturally!

You can make a rainbow right on your wall!
What colors do you see?

You need:
- A small mirror
- A clear jar filled with water
- A flashlight
- A white wall

How it works:
1. Place the mirror inside the jar.
2. Bring the jar into a dark room with white walls.
3. Turn on the flashlight and shine the light onto the mirror.
4. If you don't see a rainbow, try changing the angle of the flashlight until you do.